T. H Underwood

## Our Flag

A Poem in Four Cantos

T. H Underwood

**Our Flag**
*A Poem in Four Cantos*

ISBN/EAN: 9783337102463

Printed in Europe, USA, Canada, Australia, Japan

Cover: Foto ©Andreas Hilbeck / pixelio.de

More available books at **www.hansebooks.com**

# OUR FLAG.

## A POEM

## IN FOUR CANTOS.

BY

T. H. UNDERWOOD.

———◆•◆———

NEW YORK:

CARLETON, PUBLISHER, 413 BROADWAY.

M DCCC LXII.

DAVIES & KENT,

STEREOTYPERS AND ELECTROTYPERS,

163 *William Street, N. Y.*

# OUR FLAG.

## CANTO FIRST.

I STOOD within a graveyard old and grim;
  The lichen-bearded stones along the wall
Are browned with age, and from each ragged rim
  A copious sweat exudes.  Death hangs a pall
Of sadness where the olden sleepers lie,
And Gloom and Silence wander ever by.


In that old burial-ground the dead are strewn,
  Like autumn leaves, promiscuous and profuse;
O'er broken head-stones grass is rankly grown,
  And weeds are there, and earth-plants, whose sole use
May be to call Ambition back to earth
With mundane homilies on modest worth.

A lesson needed in this Southern clime,
　Where selfish pride, outgrowing ancient bounds,
Assumes the red-heroic, black-sublime
　Of Treason! Ah! through all those waiting grounds
Are voices murmuring curses on your name,
Who mix their glory with your present shame.


The glory of a nation has its times,
　Its changing aspects and its various modes.
Just now we mingle our heroic rhymes
　With songs of treason and phrenetic odes;
With interludes of blare and party prate,
Confusion, and a brotherhood of hate.


Not far remote a Southern town is seen,
　But little heeded in the world of rhyme;
She comes before us now with hands unclean,
　A mark of scorn for all the after time:
The nursing mother (History will say)
Of Tyranny and Treason in her day.


O Richmond! Richmond! fallen to the dust
　Is all the glory of thy former pride.
The stain is on thee of that sinful lust
　Which tears can not efface nor penance hide;
No partial history nor golden song
Can veil thee from the memory of this wrong.

Abounding in that graveyard are the urns
  Where rest the ashes of the honored dead,
Of those whose eloquence forever burns—
  A light to marvel at—a fire to dread.
Their theme was Freedom—'twas a glorious theme—
To which their slaves responded with a scream.


Close on the margin of an open grave
  A gaunt and ghastly apparition stood;
No wilder image madness ever gave,
  No form more spectral haunts that gloomy wood;
His bony arms closed on his bony breast,
His wayward head rolled in a wild unrest.


His hair, uncombed, in matted masses hung,
  As river grasses cling about a wreck;
His horrid beard, like vulture feathers, clung
  In wisps and knots about his corded neck.
The signs of madness all his body bore,
No ghastlier face a dead man ever wore.


His tattered garments hung about his hips
  And round his heels, or flaunted on the air;
No moisture was there on his parchéd lips,
  That by the fever cracked and crusted were;
His breathing hard, his speaking wild and low,
His features furrowed by some grievous woe.

His arms unclosing, o'er the grave he leaned,
 As one communing with the dead below.
The fragments of the wand'ring speech I gleaned
 Were burdens of a grief I could not know.
In words that mingled love, and hate, and dread,
He wildly thus conversed above the dead—


"Heaven's light is clouded on my soul;' and so
 I walk as in the shadow of a wing
Which hath a night of terror in it. No!
 Come not too near me, *Master;* I may spring
In my strong hate upon thy tyrant soul,
And drag it hellward to its proper goal."


His arms he wildly waved upon the air
 As one who guards himself against a foe;
He strove to fly, but something held him there;
 He struggled fiercely, but he could not go.
His bosom heaved with an oppressive weight—
The struggle seemed a contest with his fate.


A hand unseen had clutched him by the breast
 And upright held him, rigid, corpsely cold;
Far backward leaning, all his weight he pressed,
 Yet did not fall, nor could release the hold
Of that relentless grasp which held him there;
In vain his efforts and in vain his prayer.

The force unseen relaxing in its hold
  Too suddenly, a frightful impulse gave,
Which backward hurled him on the loosened mold,
  Supine and helpless, near the open grave.
Then all was silent as the house of death—
The very stillness seemed to hush its breath.


I called the sexton, and with trembling haste
  We raised the madman from his earthy bed.
He clasped the sufferer's knees, and I his waist,
  We bore him thus, as soldiers bear the dead,
With slow and labored steps, across a rill,
Up to the nearest mansion on the hill.


We laid him gently on a snowy bed;
  The linen shrank away instinctively
Beneath its ghastly burden: shrank in dread
  From rags, and dirt, and blood, and mystery.
Tenaciously the death-bed sheets retain
The spot and odor of a dead man's stain.


A fearful sight as ever met the eye
  Was that delirium-shattered wreck of man;
His facial bones projecting sharp and high;
  His arms were dwindled to a meager span:
Each joint and tendon coming to the light,
Unfleshed and rigid, horrified the sight.

The ancient sexton, garrulously wise
    In all the lore of graveyards, every mode
And aspect of the dead, showed no surprise;
    To him the scene was but an episode,
A trifle in the tragedy of life,
Where Death is hero in the mortal strife:


In all the ways of death was well informed—
    In sinapistic pharmacy was read;
And so he talked, and with his talking warmed;
    He treated me to schedules of the dead,
Whose gratitude was due for decent care
And timely rest from noise of earth and air.


"I never yet, in all the many years
    I've lived and labored for the honest dead
(For I have worked for them, and shed some tears,
    Albeit the heart may, peradventure, wed
Itself to use—may sometimes be remiss),
I never buried such a corse as this.


"I said a corse, but do not mean it such,
    Nor shall I stop the case to analyze.
He's very still, quite cold—I grant as much;
    But dead men do not plead so with their eyes.
Um! I have saved one person in my day
Whose kindred had consigned her to the clay.

"And I will tell you how it came about,
 If you have patience and the will to hear.
A stormy night it was; the lights were out;
 The winds were shrieking, ghostly, wild, and drear,
As through the vaults, with fearful roar and rave,
They called a specter from each sunken grave.


"The Lord have mercy! what a fearful night
 To walk among the tombs! On pallid stones
The ghosts were sitting, shrouded close in white,
 And all the air was filled with hollow moans.
At twelve o'clock, an hour untimely late,
There came three persons to the graveyard gate.


"Three men were they, each muffled in a cloak,
 And every face behind a curtain masked.
They shook with nervous dread, but neither spoke,
 Save one, whose husky voice an entrance asked;
Then quickly to a Gothic vault they bore
A covered corse, and laid it at the door.


"They carried it within that gloomy place;
 The lamps were lighted round the dripping wall.
The cloth removed, I saw the sweetest face
 That ever lay beneath a funeral pall;
A slumbering angel in her beauty lay,
Wrapt in the purest mold of human clay.

"The mystic silence of those muffled men
　　Awoke suspicion, and I watched their way;
No evidence of doubt could mortal then
　　Discern in me—I had my part to play.
Around the coffin kneeled the maskers three,
Then, rising slowly, left the dead with me.

"I had a clear conviction of her fate—
　　They'd brought her here to bury her alive!
I listened till I heard the closing gate
　　And rattling carriage-wheels along the drive.
My sense was sharp—I found the signs of life,
And through the storm and darkness called my wife.

"She came at once; and to our cheerful room
　　We bore the corse. We watched it through the night.
When rosy morning came, thank God! the bloom
　　Of life returned, and reason's holy light.
More perfect loveliness, through clearer eyes,
No mortal ever drew from out the skies!"

The sexton ceased; I saw his wandering eyes
　　Most strangely wink; he quickly turned his head,
And then his face evinced a wild surprise
　　To see the man sit upright on his bed;
And gazing at us, calmly and quite sane,
With not a sign of madness or of pain!

Across his bed the nation's banner lay,
  With many brilliant, emblematic stars ;
Much torn it was, and soiled with blood and clay.
  Was it a relic of illustrious wars ?
I could not tell, nor did I seek to know—
I wondered only why he clutched it so.


No word he uttered as he sat upright,
  But o'er the draggled ensign bowed his head.
His breath was softer and his eyes less bright ;
  The skin was moist where late the fever fed.
We silent sat, while he, but now so wild,
Wept audibly, like some heart-broken child.

# CANTO SECOND.

"Come closer, now, and hold that banner near;
　You see a stain! well, that is human blood;
Ay, human blood! Now sit you down and hear
　How came it there. The tale will do some good,
If it but teaches you to hate that rag—
To call down curses on that lying flag.


"Some fifteen years ago, or thereaway,
　Out West I lived, in that far better land
Where luckless bondmen do not wear away
　Their lives so quick beneath the tyrant's hand;
But even there I've heard such cries of pain
As made the blood stand still in every vein.


"Saint Louis was the city where I dwelt—
　Its wealth and wit are not unknown to fame—
A Western town, and yet I've seen and felt
　Such crimes that I have learned to curse its name.
Ah! God forgive me! I have wished His fire
Or plague would blast it with unmeasured ire.

"They called me Varney's Jeff (for JEFFERSON
  My mother christened me, I know not why;
Perhaps in mockery, for there was one
  You reverence now, who wrote a brilliant *lie*—
A LIE self-evident, our masters say;
They hate him well, and, hating, we obey).


"For Colonel Varney held me as his own,
  Though I was comely and as white as he;
My soul was his, my muscle, flesh, and bone—
  And with his mules and swine he counted me.
'Twas said my face some hated secret told;
I could not help it—nature will be bold.


"I have his nose—a marked, peculiar nose—
  I have the same proud curling of the lip;
His brilliant eye that like a diamond glows,
  His form, his face, except the faintest dip
Of Afric tinge, which in my mother run,
I am in all things Colonel Varney's son.


"My mother was his slave, an Octoroon;
  Her eyes were blue, her face Caucasian fair.
He bought her for his wife, at honey-moon,
  A proper gift, to watch her sleeping-chair,
Her couch and bed, in petulance and pain—
In short, to be the Hebe of her train.

" Her name was Lucy (master called her Loo),
  A model woman, rounded in her flesh ;
To maiden trust she ever had been true ;
  Thus all her beauty keeping pure and fresh.
This Varney saw, and, gloating o'er her charms,
Resolved to bring her to his lech'rous arms.


" My mistress was a sweet-faced, marble saint,
  As white as linen, passionless and cold ;
And Varney's love for her had grown so faint,
  He laid it by as something worn and old.
Such gallant men their dark Delilahs keep,
And in the lap of lust lie down to sleep.


" He forced my mother, helpless, to his room,
  And she became the thing she hated most ;
Her beauty vanished, and the health and bloom
  Forsook her face—her only light was lost.
To hide his shame when I, his son, was born,
He treated her with cruelty and scorn.


" My master sported epaulets and plume,
  He dangled at his thigh a jeweled sword ;
And like a hero he could fret and fume,
  Take attitude, and mouth a martial word.
The people called him COLONEL VARNEY then,
And he was honored much and praised of men.

"There came a day, eventful, dreadful day!
    It brought rejoicing and a roll of drums.
The streets were hung with banners floating gay;
    The people shouted, ' Lo ! the hero comes!
Puissant Varney ! none so great as he !
Let cannon speak the nation's jubilee !'


"This hated flag I held that gala morn ;
    My gentle mistress placed it in my hand ;
' Your master will be pleased to see it borne
    So bravely by his Jeff—'tis very grand.'
She said it cheerfully, but all the while
The artless tears stood wond'ring at her smile.


" Arranged were all the servants in a row,
    And each a flag, with martial roses drest
They stood, like puppets well disposed for show,
    A star and badge and ribbon on each breast.
Our saintly mistress looked as pure and pale
As marble Isis, covered with her veil.


" The street was crowded, and the pavement lined
    With crinoline and puffery and pride;
The wild huzzas grew louder on the wind,
    From cavalry and footmen, far and wide ;
And, moving onward, high in martial fame,
Great Colonel Varney like a hero came.

"Our mistress marked him bowing left and right;
   And as he nearer came she paler grew—
The pageantry grew dimmer on her sight;
   Then all the vision faded from her view—
And then she sat as still and white as death;
No witness gave of moving pulse or breath.


"The long procession halted at the door,
   And Colonel Varney, from his sudden throne,
Descended proudly 'mid the clamorous roar,
   And blasts of triumph by the bugle blown.
Then all the people hailed him with a shout,
And opened wide a passage in his route.


"He mounted then the marble steps, in reach,
   But all unmindful of his fainting wife;
Then faced the crowd, and, in a swelling speech,
   Re-consecrated all his after-life
To liberty, his country, and his GOD—
A thousand lips the mockery applaud.


"He stood within the wide and cheerless hall,
   With rattling sheath and war-boots iron heeled,
With blood-red plume that swept the upper wall,
   As carnage sweeps ambition's battle-field;
With air sardonic marched into his room,
Where he could storm at will, and fret and fume.

" 'Here, Jeff, you rascal, draw these scoundrel boots!
Here, Washington, unbuckle this damn'd sword!
Wine! water! quicker, you infernal coots!
I'll kill the first black wretch that thinks a word—
Who dares exceed my wish, or render less—
I'm not a marvel in my tenderness.'


" 'Here, Lucy! ah, you Afric Lachesis!
What means this show of blacks, with flags and stars?
Who improvised a greeting such as this?
A he-goat regiment to welcome Mars!'
Poor Lucy quailed beneath his angry eye;
And, fearing for her mistress, answered, ' I.'


" 'Begone! you wench!' he shouted, fierce and high;
And Lucy, frightened, hurried from the room.
'That wench conceals a secret in this lie—
She can not brush *me* with a silver broom.
There is a way to move my marble wife,
And I will use it though it cost a life.'


" Just then I saw him drop into his boot
A bunch of keys—I thought by accident.
Ah, GOD! too soon I learned the martial brute
A fearful purpose by that action meant;
A fiendish murder followed it that day,
The thought of which has made me early gray.

" 'Twas four o'clock, and wild confusion reigned
    Through all the house—fierce oaths and angry words
Came down to us who to this brute were chained;
    We knew the omen, and, like fettered birds,
We fluttered in our cages, one and all;
Not knowing when or where the storm would fall.


" The tyrant's voice rose boisterously high,
    And echoed hoarsely through the hollow room;
' My keys! you thief! now find them, or you die!
    By God, I'll lash you till the crack of doom!
You leman hag, I'll teach you now that I
Am not the victim of your foolish lie.'


" I heard the furious stamping of a heel,
    And saw the brute, with unrelenting air,
Assault his wife with force that made her reel,
    And clutch my mother rudely by the hair;
With violence he dragged her to the door,
And thence his victim to the stable bore.


" He stript her naked, bound her to a stall,
    Tied ropes about her hands, her feet, her hair,
Then locked the door.  I heard my mistress call:
    ' Jeff! Jeff!'  In haste I mounted up the stair,
But sudden stopt—there rose the wildest cry
That ever startled hell or shocked the sky.

"More like a corpse than anything of life,
 Save in her moanings and her face of fear,
Prone on a pallet lay the shivering wife,
 Her nervous palm pressed vainly to her ear;
She vainly strove to stop the dreadful sound—
It pierced her soul, as arrows pierce a wound.


"'O master! master!—God! O *God!* O GOD!
 O! O! O!—help me, missus!—help me, do!
Do spare me, master! mercy! mercy! GOD!'
 The fearful cries went stinging through and through
Her frightened soul.  She started from her bed,
And, wildly screaming, down the stairway fled.


"In vain her hands assail the heavy door—
 Poor wasted hands, they had no power to save—
In vain did she with earnest lips implore
 Her brutal husband—vainly weep and rave:
''Twas I! 'twas I!  Oh, kill me, too!' she cried;
'Come out and do a double homicide!'


"A scornful laugh was all the fiend replied;
 And then the work went on with sterner will—
With quicker hand the deadly lash he plied—
 The shrieks were changed to moans, then all was still.
The fainting wife fell forward with a groan,
And gashed her temple on the sill of stone.

"Enough of this; I leave the rest with God,
   Who then beheld and suffered this great sin.
These crimson spots are my poor mother's blood;
   This was the winding sheet I wrapt her in,
When, in the night, I stole her corpse away
To give it rest within its house of clay.


"We bore our mistress lifeless to her room,
   And, for a moment, weeping, round her stood;
From thence they took her to her peaceful tomb;
   God rest her spirit—she was kind and good.
No purer mortal ever walked the ground—
No brighter spirit have the angels crowned.


"The murder made me frantic, and my ways
   To him were troublesome.  One course was left:
He sold me South—then came the crushing days
   Of crime and cruelty, which have bereft
My soul of hope through years of weary time—
The end was madness and a double crime.


"With chains, and whips, and mockery oppressed,
   The soul and body wither—year by year.
My Southern master gave me little rest;
   My education was his staple sneer;
The doubtful color of my face, so white,
Provoked his rage, malevolence, and spite.

# CANTO THIRD.

" 'Twas yesterday," he said, "and yet to me
   A moment only seems the vanished day—
A maniac dream of clouds and stormy sea—
   A sigh, a groan, and all has passed away!
No matter now; regret will not avail;
The sum of life is but an infant's wail.


" A ghastly face, a form all gashed and grim—
   My murdered WIFE is pleading near me now;
I see her bleeding breast and mangled limb,
   Her lacerated neck and welted brow,
And he who murdered her is at her side,
A spectral form of cruelty and pride.


" His smile is wicked, such as all men know
   In pictures of the father of all lies.
I met him yesterday; his brows were low;
   Two hissing snakes were couchant in his eyes.
He said to me, ' You have been preaching, *Cuff*,
Your Abolition heresies and stuff.

" 'Bah! you are fed until you're grown too fat;
    Your cloth is quite too fine—you are too proud!
Be careful, Jeff; I'll have no more of that—
    Be satisfied, more circumspect, less loud!
The law is vigilant and rife in ways,
And for your servile class has no delays!


" 'I give you Christian home, and clothes, and food;
    What further kindness can you ask of me?
A base return is your ingratitude—
    A silly figment is your Liberty.
No care have you, no debts, no factious duns;
Your life an easy, even tenure runs.'


"I answered him: 'In all the good you name
    Your sires were blest—in property and limbs;
To wives and children had unquestioned claim—
    Were masters of their wishes and their whims;
And yet they shed their blood right liberally
For this same silly figment, Liberty!


" 'Did English masters bind you with a chain,
    And buy and sell you in the market-place?
Or did they ship you, hopeless, o'er the main,
    Or brand their names upon your back and face,
Or roast you while your bleeding wounds were fresh,
Or tear, and saw, and gash your quivering flesh?

" ' Did they forbid you, under pain of death,
    To read the Bible and to worship God?
No! all was free as sun and summer breath—
    In fancy only did you feel the rod.
O Christ! O God! if those have called to Thee,
How much more claim upon such help have we?'


"He frowned upon me with his lips and eyes,
    In icy, haughty attitude of hate;
In every line his features said, 'Despise!'
    In every sneer a mocking devil sate;
And there he stood, a tyrant, self-elect,
A scornful statue, rigidly erect.


"He, frowning, said, 'You tread forbidden ground;
    The old Apostles did not agitate;
They preached the gospel, and were never found
    As brawling intermeddlers in the state.
Such doctrines only as are lawful teach,
For this you're set apart by *us* to preach.'


"And I replied: 'They did not agitate?
    They surely did, but they were few and weak;
The legal harpies of the church and state
    Environed them, the lowly and the meek—
Pursued them ever, with malignant ire,
To loathsome caverns or through blood and fire.

" ' Yet they have come to rule the world anew,
　　And, in their turn, oppress the weaker class.
The old Apostles are renewed in you,
　　And GOD has willed that it should come to pass.
Appalling truth!　Beware! for HE is just—
HE holds our recompense, and come it must!'

" Again his brow came downward like a cloud;
　　His muttered curses, under breath, I heard;
I bore myself, perhaps, a little proud.
　　I saw my master's deepest hate was stirred,
For, sneering wickedly, he shook his head,
And, with a sharp malignity, he said: ·

" ' Accursed be Canaan! on her rests the rod!
　　Her sons and daughters to the latest breath.
This condemnation, thus announced by GOD,
　　Is bondage, unconditional as death.
Christ ratified it, and with lip and pen
The Christian churches have replied, " Amen!" '

" I boldly answered: ' 'Tis a shameless fraud
　　Upon the common sense of all the world!
A blasphemy—a crime against our GOD,
　　Which Christian nations of the earth have hurled
Back in your teeth—the argument of knaves
Who have their interest in holding slaves!

" ' And even this great nation feels the crime
That dims the luster of her gleaming stars—
That clouds the sunshine of the fairest clime
Of all the earth—and her avenging Mars
Is rushing Southward with his battle-cry,
And, in the onset, Slavery must die


" ' E'en now the winds are vocal with the shout
Of ransomed men, who leap as from the grave,
Who weep and pray, and throw their arms about,
And float on FREEDOM as upon a wave !
They kneel in rapture now, and kiss the earth,
And shout hosannahs to their second birth.'


" And then my master, softening, blandly said :
' Your tongue is eloquent—so, so, I see !
Your wife is feeble, you are gently bred—
To-day your wife, to-morrow you are free.' .
I knelt and blest him, lowly bent my head,
And wept the sweetest tears I ever shed.


" With buoyant step and happy heart I went
To every duty master set for me.
I worked and sang until the day was spent,
And many times I dropt upon my knee,
Imploring blessings on my master there,
In earnest, truthful, and devoted prayer.

I then went homeward, singing with great joy,
     'I shall be FREE! my wife no more a slave!
With nothing now to mar our bliss, Namoi.
     Free! free! Now let your glorious banner wave!
For it is beautifully clear to me—
No longer now a frightful mystery.'


"Deprive the world of light for one long year,
     Let all men live despairingly in gloom
Till eyes grow useless, and all hearts grown scar
     Cry out for rest and riddance in the tomb;
Then open heaven, let the sweet light shine,
And you would see a rapture such as mine.


"'O joy! O bliss! O light of that new day!'
     I laughed, I sang, I shouted 'LIBERTY!'
I ran, I leapt, as light and young as May—
     That new sensation was no mystery.
Near by my cabin waved that banner free;
I ran to call my darling out to see.


"With eager haste I opened wide the door
     And called to her. She neither moved nor spoke.
I called again; I thumped upon the floor—
     No other sound upon the stillness broke.
With quick impatience to her side I flew—
Saw!—sickened and appalled, I backward drew!

"Ah, God! a chill of horror seized my joints!
  I stood stone-still, blood oozing from my lips—
I dimly saw a hundred wiry points
  Play round my wife, on bloody, spectral whips,
And each fell point plowed deep into my heart
With anguish such as no flesh-wounds impart.


"O'er all her face I saw great ridges rise;
  Like fiery snakes they coiled about her throat—
They strangled me, they darted at my eyes,
  And with their fangs the burning eyeballs smote.
Large, quivering welts were creeping, red and black,
With bloody scales, along her naked back.


"The deep-cut furrows of the steel-thong'd whips,
  Red-rimmed and raw and open to the air,
Plowed through her bosom and along her hips,
  Unfleshed the sinews, and the bones laid bare.
No word she uttered, neither curse nor prayer,
Nor wept, nor moaned, nor seemed to heed me there.


"Then through my brain, with hot, impatient heels,
  Trooped the damned brotherhood of tyranny!
I heard blasphemous shouts and laughter peals
  In mockery of Freedom.  Sneeringly
The scoffers taunted me with chain and rod,
And bade me call upon the Negro's God!

" In trembling eagerness I drew a stool
    Close to my dying wife, some water brought
To bathe her bleeding wounds, and strove to cool
    The deadly fever that the whips had wrought.
But all my efforts and my tears were vain
To soothe the body's or the spirit's pain.


" She suffered much, but did not suffer long—
    The murd'rous hands had done their work too well;
The thirsty lash, with sharp, steel-pointed thong,
    Too skillfully had opened that deep cell
Where Life, imprisoned, waits the coming time,
Nor asks who knocks—disease, or age, or crime.


" Her face was lovely as she turned to me,
    The light of heaven beaming in her eye;
She faintly said, ' Rejoice, for I am free !'
    Her life went out.   Oh! do not ask me why
I shouted ' Joy !'   I felt sublimely brave,
For she I clasped was mine, and no man's slave.


" And thus my master kept his word with me—
    His fiendish promise given yesterday—
' Your wife is feeble, I will set her free ;'
    And mine, of course, will come without delay.
I know not how, nor care I to inquire—
Enough ! 'tis welcome, be it rope or fire.

"A bruiséd corse now lay upon my bed,
  In bloody garments, torn of brutal hands.
More beautiful to me my mangled dead
  Than in the morning of our nuptial bands,
For now my darling in her slumber lay
As royally as lies the noblest clay.


"Not far remote, a tall and branchless tree,
  In brave defiance wagg'd its haughty head,
And on its summit, floating far and free,
  Your nation's ensign to the breeze was spread;
The emblem of a covenant with hell,
Across my door its hateful shadow fell.


"The blessed privilege is ours to dwell
  Beneath its shade, to count our welts and scars,
To have you cram us in the throat of hell
  With songs of freedom and a show of stars.
Hypocrisy! legitimate of crime,
Thy parent bred thee in this Southern clime.


"'Twas late at night, when all the world was still,
  Among the buried 'whites' I dug her grave;
I made a box—the best my awkward skill
  Could furnish her, for I was but a slave.
The coffin first, and then my wife, I bore
To that rude grave, and laid her at its door. .

"A long, long hour I wept above her head—
　　I could not, would not give her to the tomb;
I talked with her as though she were not dead,
　　Forgetting time, and loneliness, and gloom.
I talked to her of vengeance, and it seemed
She answered me!   Alas! my spirit dreamed!


"I said 'good-bye,' and laid her in her bed,
　　With rapid hands filled in the rattling clod;
I spread a quilt of turf above her head,
　　Then kissed the grave and left her with her GOD.
Then all the earth was desolate to me,
I helpless lay as on a shoreless sea.


"Some demon led me to my hut again—
　　His hand of fire illumined all the way;
The light, intensive, burned into my brain,
　　And made the darkness lighter than the day.
Mysterious lips, articulate and clear,
Came round me, whisp'ring 'Vengeance!' in my ear.


"A heavy knife, once used for cutting cane,
　　Lay in my cupboard, still and waitingly;
I called to it, nor did I call in vain—
　　It answered sharply, 'I am here for thee!'
So we together, confident of right,
Went on a mission in that moonless night.

"I found the overseer, debauched with wine,
　Serenely sleeping in his lecherous bed,
And in his arms a negro concubine,
　Whose breast, perforce, sustained his tyrant head.
The knife said, 'Die?' I answered, 'Yes!' He died,
Nor stirred the woman sleeping at his side.


"The next, my master, he who planned the deed—
　I found him drinking with a neighbor-friend;
I watched him late, of all his ways took heed,
　For well I knew his revelry would end
In drunkenness, and, reckless of the night,
He'd stagger home with neither guide nor light.


"I saw him coming, met him at the gate,
　But under cover hid myself away.
I followed him remorselessly as Fate;
　He reached a wood that on his journey lay—
There by the throat I held him to the ground,
And through his heart I made a ghastly wound.


"Then I returned to that old burial-place,
　And laid me down upon my darling's grave.
I moaned, and wept, and fell upon my face;
　I called her name—the tomb no answer gave.
A maniac dream came o'er my spirit then—
A dream of hounds and hard, relentless men.

"They came, with gun, and rope, and whip, and chain,
   To capture me, and I in terror fled!
Long hours I fled—they seemed a year of pain—
   Around and round that waste-field of the dead.
Each sunken grave a pool of carnage seemed,
And from the head-stones blood in torrents streamed.


"They grappled me, those spectral men and hounds,
   With whips and teeth they tore my flesh away;
My feverish ears were filled with horrid sounds,
   And all the night was luminous as day.
The ghastly people of the graves came out,
And mocked, and jeered, and shuffled me about.


"I heard my wife, imprison'd in her cell,
   Cry out for help!  O! then a demon's might
Strung every sinew, all the fires of hell
   Flashed through my blood, and till the morning light,
With rapid hands, I tore the earth away,
In haste to dig her from the smothering clay.


"But round me closed the unrelenting men;
   They grasped me by the breast and by the throat;
They held me upright for a moment, then
   With heavy hands my throbbing temples smote.
The rest was darkness.  I awaken here,
My madness over and my reason clear.

"I know not why this flag I still retain,
  But well I know it haunts me to my doom;
In all that night of horror and of pain
  I dragged the hated banner through the gloom;
The curse pursues me with a demon-spell,
As devils haunt a guilty soul through hell!


"So much of me; and now of others hear
  The frightful secret of that lady's life,
Revealed this morning, fell upon my ear
  Appallingly.  'Tis well my bloody knife
Was her avenging angel ere I knew
How deep in sin were steeped the knaves it slew.


"Of those three men the principals were two—
  My master and his scoundrel overseer—
Myself the third.  I thought their statements true,
  Believed her dead, and wept above her bier.
I mourned for her, she was so young and fair;
Much wronged she was, as Southern women are.


"Her death was sudden, and her large estate
  Became my master's; here the secret lies.
A reckless man he was, defying fate,
  And held 'the means the purpose justifies'—
A villain maxim which your laws advise,
Which rascals practice, honest men despise."

He sudden ceased, for on the winds without
　A sound of voices broke upon the ear.
Below the window rose a savage shout—
　A clamor loud, tumultuous, and near,
And then the tramping of a thousand feet
Awoke the echoes all along the street.


The mob was there, and clamorous for blood;
　A storm of angry curses swept the stair;
The rabble, pouring inward like a flood,
　Rushed thro' the hall-way, screaming, "He is there!"
They dashed the door and swarmed into the room,
And dragged the helpless victim to his doom.


They tossed him from the window to the street—
　He fell among the rioters below,
Who caught him up and set him on his feet,
　And hustled him along, with many a blow,
Through lanes of mockers, armed with whips and brands;
He fell, was dragged, or crawled upon his hands.

# CANTO FOURTH.

Ring out, O bells! the Nation's Sabbath-day!
   The glorious Fourth! Ye people, clap your hands!
Hang up your banners! (hide the chains away;)
   Let "Freedom" sound o'er all these goodly lands!
What matter if our gallant ensign waves
Above the fetters of four million slaves!


Drums, beat your rataplans! shrill-screaming fife,
   Shriek "Hail Columbia" with relentless air!
Let shouts and bonfires mix in friendly strife
   With anthems loud and patriotic prayer.
Hoarse-throated cannon call unto the sea!
Four million slaves may answer "jubilee."


Our nation's ensign bravely cuts the sky—
   Its stars are flashing from their lofty height!
Down, busy devil—your suggestive lie,
   Expediency will cover from the sight.
Hint not of "slaves," but shout the "glorious cause,"
The "Constitution!" "Declaration!" "Laws!"

Ha! here is one who in his fetters stands—
   The truth will out—he standeth here a SLAVE;
Strong ropes are knotted on his neck and hands;
   'Tis said he dies the death that knows no grave—
The death of deaths—appalling death of fire!
His feet are planted on his funeral pyre.


The staff that lifts our banner to the sky
   Is now his stake—his arms are pinioned there,
Above his head, and painfully too high—
   (The scorners say, "an attitude of prayer.")
Chains round the staff and round his body twine,
And to the "sacred pole" his limbs confine.


Here are three men, whose manhood is unknown
   In Heaven's court, three men of vulgar speech,
And faces hard, by evil passions grown
   To vulpine hideousness.  They're holding each
A pine-wood torch; in readiness they stand
To vindicate the honor of their land!


The ruffian mob in thousands gather round—
   The wolfish pack who dragged him through the street.
They torture him with many a grievous wound—
   His body flay, and burn his hands and feet.
Sublimely silent, he awaits his death
With brow serene and even-tenured breath.

A "man of God" (the blasphemy I write
   To show what brute-depravity has done
To sacred things), in ministerial white,
   Is standing here.  How glib his tongue does run
With libels on his country and his time!
He calls on GOD to sanctify this crime!


Repeats the standard falsehoods of his class;
   Is flush in Bible saws and legal lore;
Is rich in sophistry of sounding brass,
   In reasons blatant.  With a pious roar
He deals anathemas on seed of Ham,
And curses Canaan with an unctuous damn.


This priest of Baäl by the victim stands,
   Parades his learning and his lust as well.
In holy horror, and with lifted hands,
   Consigns all Abolitionists to hell—
Belabors Freedom with the Holy Writ,
Then goes his way pedantic of his wit.


The torchmen then apply their ready match,
   And soon the blaze assails the victim's feet.
Wild laughter rises, as the faggots catch,
   In approbation.  From each lane and street
The human tide rolls onward in its ire
To swell the horrid carnival of fire.

The pitchy pine the native instinct shows
    For negro flesh to feed its appetite.
In flaming fury now it leaps and glows,
    And closing round him shuts him from the sight.
A laugh of triumph is the only sound
That gives report of him to those around.


Right over this baptismal font of fire
    Most haughtily the nation's colors wave!
The shoutings of the mob reach high—but higher
    The upward-leaping laughter of the slave—
A laugh of joy! the soul's loud jubilee,
As it goes up, through flames. to Heaven, FREE!


Now upward springing from its human feast,
    The unabating, angry blaze assaults
The towering staff, and like a growling beast
    Climbs up the wood and on the banner vaults;
Its fiery fangs the shiv'ring ensign clasp
And crisp and curl it in their envious grasp!


They clutch it close, and hold it shriv'ling there;
    They fiercely pluck each glittering star away!
Ah, GOD! a flag of fire floats on the air,
    Grows *red*, then *black*, and parting from its stay,
An instant waves a pirate rag, and, lo!
It falls to ashes on the mob below!

'Tis emblematic of a nation's thrall,
　And of the doom that His good time will bide;
In blood and fire shall her red fetters fall,
　And she arise, redeemed and purified.
The conquering Right will leave to after time
The giant CINDER of a giant CRIME.

www.ingramcontent.com/pod-product-compliance
Lightning Source LLC
Chambersburg PA
CBHW061238260626
47172CB00003B/917